# The
# ROSE
# BOWL

Published by Creative Education, Inc.

123 South Broad Street, Mankato, MN 56001

Designed by Rita Marshall with the help of Thomas Lawton

Cover illustration by Rob Day, Lance Hidy Associates

Copyright © 1993 by Creative Education, Inc.

Photography by Allsport, Mel Bailey, Duomo,
Pasadena Tournament of Roses, Spectra-Action,
Sports Illustrated (Peter Miller), Wide World Photos

Printed in the United States

Library of Congress Cataloging-in-Publication Data

Deegan, Paul J., 1937–

The Rose Bowl / Paul Deegan.

p.   cm.—(Great moments in sports)

Summary: Presents "great" moments from college football
games played at the Rose Bowl Stadium in Pasadena every
January 1 since 1902.

ISBN 0-88682-534-2

1. Rose Bowl Game, Pasadena, Calif.—History—Juvenile
literature.   [1. Rose Bowl Game, Pasadena, Calif.—History.
2. Football—History.]   I. Title.   II. Series.        92-3723

GV957.R6D44   1992                                      CIP

796.332′63′0979493—dc20                                 AC

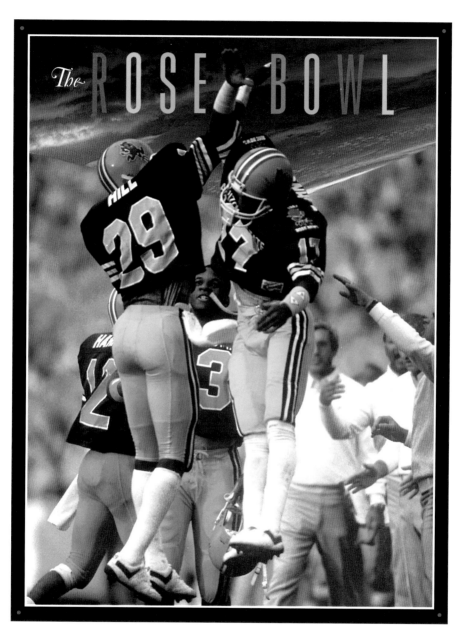

# The ROSE BOWL

PAUL DEEGAN

CREATIVE EDUCATION INC.

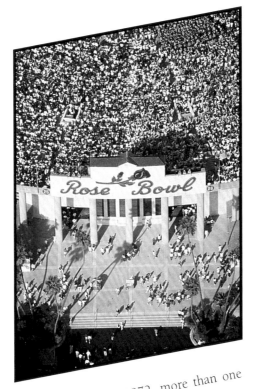

On the first day of 1972, more than one hundred thousand fans filled the Rose Bowl Stadium in Pasadena. They were there to watch the annual Rose Bowl game, one of college football's most exciting events and the granddaddy of all bowl tournaments. The fans expected a great game—and they weren't disappointed.

Representing the Big Ten were the University of Michigan Wolverines. Opposing them was the Stanford University Cardinal from the Pac-10 Conference. Stanford was a decided underdog, but, as all football fans know, upsets are part of the tradition of the Rose Bowl game.

A determined Stanford team battled the Wolverines on an even basis through fifty-eight minutes of play. But, with less than two minutes in the game, the Cardinal still trailed 12-10.

Though Stanford now had the ball, the team was seventy-eight yards from the Michigan goal line. It was a tough situation, but the gritty Stanford offense had no intention of giving up.

*The Wolverines faced Arizona State in 1987.*

Cardinal quarterback Don Bunce crouched behind his center, snapping out his cadence. Bunce knew this series of downs would determine whether or not Stanford could pull off the upset of the season and produce one of the greatest moments in Rose Bowl history. Stanford needed at least a field goal; if the Pac-10 team had to give up the ball without scoring, the Big Ten champions would win the game.

*Iowa fell to Washington, 28–0, in the 1982 game.*

Since its inception just after the turn of the century, the Rose Bowl football game has provided fans with many great contests, outstanding players, and memorable moments.

✱ During the 1926 game, the University of Alabama scored three touchdowns, one on a fifty-nine-yard pass, in the first seven minutes of the third quarter. This scoring explosion gave the Crimson Tide a 20-19 victory over the University of Washington in what some say was the best Rose Bowl contest ever.

✱ In the waning moments of the 1949 game, a trick play gave Northwestern University a 20-14 upset victory over the University of California. The snap from center went past the quarterback to the Wildcats' deep back, Frank Aschenbrenner, who ran forty-three yards for the winning touchdown.

✱ In the 1990 Rose Bowl game, USC marched seventy-five yards for the winning touchdown in a 17-10 victory over Michigan. In the final minutes of the game, a fake punt by Michigan was negated by a holding penalty, forcing the Wolverines to punt to USC. The Trojans then began their winning drive.

*Michigan running back Leroy Hoard.*

The Rose Bowl football game is the climax of the Tournament of Roses, an annual celebration that takes place in Pasadena, California. Besides the football game, one of its main attractions is a nationally televised parade that features beautiful flower-covered floats. Each year Pasadena, a community of about 120,000 in the greater Los Angeles metropolitan area, attracts more than two million visitors during the Tournament of Roses. Former U.S. president Ronald Reagan—also a former governor of California—called the festival "truly one of the living wonders of the West."

*Michigan State versus USC, 1988.*

Rockne had developed a system he called the "Shock Troops." At the beginning of a game, he started his second team, letting them fight off the opponent's first charges. When he felt the opponent had tired a little, he brought his first team into the game. But this time the strategy didn't work. As the 1925 Rose Bowl got underway, the underdog Cardinal took an early lead, kicking a field goal after recovering a Notre Dame fumble. Rockne was forced to put his first team on the field earlier than he'd expected.

Notre Dame soon got back into the game with what one sportswriter called "perhaps the most beautiful bit of downfield blocking ever seen in Rose Bowl history." Miller, Layden, and the entire Notre Dame line blocked as Crowley swung to his right from their twenty-yard line. Stanford finally chased Crowley down at midfield.

*A breakaway run generates excitement among Rose Bowl fans.*

Another Crowley run, a Stuhldreher-to-Miller pass, and an eleven-yard scamper by Miller put the ball inside the Stanford ten-yard line. The Stanford line held the Fighting Irish off, however, and Notre Dame could not score.

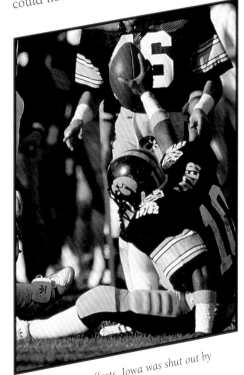

*Despite their best efforts, Iowa was shut out by Washington in 1982.*

But Stanford was forced to punt the ball back to Notre Dame, and a short kick gave the midwestern team the ball on Stanford's thirty-two-yard line. Two plays into the second quarter, Layden picked up short yardage for the score. The extra point attempt was blocked. Notre Dame led 6-3.

A few minutes later, Layden made the defensive play of the game. (Players played both offense and defense in those days.) Ernie Nevers had pounded down the field before Stanford faced a fourth and long from the Notre Dame thirty-one-yard line. Nevers tried to cross up the defense with a pass. But Layden read the play and tipped Nevers's pass, then ran under the tipped ball and caught it. Layden never looked back, going seventy-eight yards for a touchdown. This time the extra point was made and Notre Dame's lead increased to 13-6.

Again Stanford drove into Notre Dame territory. But the Cardinal fumbled the ball at the Irish seventeen to end the first half.

Trying to narrow the margin, Stanford missed two third-period field goal attempts. Then disaster struck the West Coast team. Layden launched a fifty-yard punt that Stanford could not field. A Notre Dame lineman picked up the ball and took it into the end zone. Crowley placed the kick, and the situation began to look desperate for Stanford, now trailing 20-3.

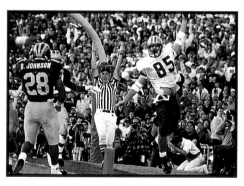

*A scoring celebration.*

*Every Rose Bowl is a hard-fought competition.*

But Nevers and his teammates certainly weren't going to quit. Nevers intercepted a Stuhldreher pass, then carried the ball to near the Irish goal time after time. Stanford finally scored on a pass and made the extra point. Now the Cardinal was only behind 20-10 with over a quarter to play.

*Northwestern defeated California in 1949.*

In the final period, Stanford intercepted another pass and took the ball inside the Irish ten-yard line. The Cardinal had first and goal from the six. But on the fourth down, over Coach Warner's protests, the referee ruled that Nevers was stopped short of the end zone. Notre Dame could breathe easier.

*Turnovers can make or break a game.*

Stanford attacked once more, only to be intercepted by Crowley, who picked off a Nevers pass at the Notre Dame ten-yard line.

As the game wound down, Nevers again tried to throw past Layden. Again Layden intercepted. And again he ran for a touchdown, his third of the day, this time going seventy yards. The extra point was made and the final score was 27-10.

The Four Horsemen had ridden again.

## WRONG WAY RIEGELS

The most famous run in Rose Bowl history took place on New Year's Day, 1929, and earned lineman Roy Riegels a nickname he would never live down—"Wrong Way" Riegels.

Riegels was a center on the 1928 University of California team and had been elected captain for the next season. His Golden Bears were facing an undefeated "Rambling Wreck" from Georgia Tech University.

In the second quarter of a scoreless game, a Tech running back fumbled the ball when tackled by California halfback Benny Lom. The ball bounced into Riegels's hands on the Tech thirty-five-yard line. Under the rules at that time, a player could run with a recovered fumble, so Riegels immediately headed with the ball for the Tech goal line.

*Pages 20–21: The 1987 celebration begins for Arizona State.*

*An Iowa player tries to force Washington to fumble in the 1991 game.*

Suddenly he pivoted to escape being tackled. He was still running hard. But he was headed for the California goal line some sixty yards away. He was running the wrong way!

His teammates automatically kept knocking down Tech players, clearing the path for the wrong-way runner. Lom, however, who had made the tackle causing the fumble, figured out what was going on. He ran after Riegels, screaming at him to stop. But Lom could not be heard over the roar of seventy-one thousand fans.

Lom kept up his desperate chase and finally caught up with Riegels inside the California ten-yard line. He reached for his teammate and managed to turn him around just before he went into the end zone. Riegels was tackled at the Georgia Tech one-yard line.

The stunned California team decided to punt out of danger on the first down. But Georgia Tech blocked the kick out of the end zone for a safety, giving Tech a 2-0 lead. A fifteen-yard touchdown run in the third quarter gave Tech an 8-0 lead.

Riegels tried to put his costly mistake out of his mind and played hard the rest of the game. He blocked a Tech punt, leading to a Golden Bears score on a pass from

*Roy Riegels's wrong-way run.*

Lom. But California did not make the extra point and lost the game to Georgia Tech with a final score of 8-7.

Riegels's perseverance in the face of misfortune did not go unnoticed, however. After the game, Georgia Tech's All-America center Peter Pund said Riegels was the best center he'd played against all year. "He's a battler, and he never quit," Pund said.

Riegels later became a successful businessman. "I gained true understanding of life from my Rose Bowl mistake," he said years later. "I learned you can bounce back from a misfortune. . . ."

One of the best offensive displays ever seen on a football field took place during the second quarter of the 1935 Rose Bowl game. The Crimson Tide of Alabama was the nation's number-one team. Three star players had helped them achieve their 10-0 record: quarterback Dixie Howell and ends Paul Bryant and Don Hutson. Bryant later became a well-known college football coach, while Hutson went on to professional stardom with the Green Bay Packers.

*The UCLA squad prepares for the 1986 classic.*

23

*USC has won more Rose Bowl games than any other team.*

Stanford University was making the second of three straight appearances in the Rose Bowl game. The team was known as the "Vow Boys" because, as freshmen, the members promised they would never lose to USC. It was a promise they kept.

Stanford was a decided underdog in this match, however. The Cardinal players knew the Tide was unbeaten, but they ran onto the field determined to win the game anyway. They took control in the first quarter and earned a 7-0 lead. Their aggressive defense stunned the potent Tide offense and Alabama gained only four yards in the entire quarter.

But Alabama's Dixie Howell, the slinger from the South, couldn't be stopped forever. The Tide rally began in the second quarter as Howell's passes moved the team down the field. Then Howell himself somersaulted into the end zone for a touchdown. But the Alabama kicker missed the conversion and the Tide was still behind by one point.

*Dixie Howell.*

So Howell again put the football in the air and drove Alabama deep into Stanford territory. The result was a twenty-two-yard field goal and a 9-7 lead for the Crimson Tide. Howell then proved that he could produce on the ground, too. He stunned the eighty-five thousand fans by racing sixty-seven yards for a touchdown.

*Jamie Morris of Michigan sprints toward the goal.*

*Arizona quarterback Jeff van Raaphorst helped lead his team to victory in 1987.*

Alabama got the ball again in the second quarter, and Howell went back to the air. He found Hutson open and the pass to his receiver resulted in a fifty-four-yard touchdown play. It was the third time in the quarter that Howell had had a hand in scoring a touchdown. The Crimson Tide had scored twenty-two points to take the halftime lead.

The Alabama quarterback wasn't finished, however. In the fourth quarter, Howell again connected with Hutson for a touchdown pass to make the final score 29-13 in favor of the Alabama team.

*Michigan defeated Washington, 23–6, in the 1981 contest.*

At the game's end, Howell had 160 yards passing on nine of twelve completions and 111 yards rushing. His performance inspired Grantland Rice to write, "Dixie Howell, the human howitzer from Hartford, Alabama, blasted the Rose Bowl dreams of Stanford with one of the greatest all-around exhibitions that football has ever known."

*Michigan's legendary coach, Bo Schembechler.*

## A TROJAN GAMBLE

The crowd that filled the Rose Bowl Stadium on the first day of 1975 expected to see a dazzling running display. On one side of the field, USC had an All-America back in Anthony Davis. On the other side, Ohio State's Archie Griffin was not only an All-American but the Heisman Trophy winner as well.

Football games don't often go as expected, however. Davis left the game with an injury in the second quarter. And the USC Trojans did a good job of defending against the elusive Griffin. When the game ended, he would have less than one hundred yards rushing for the first time in twenty-three games.

It would take a few different players to provide fans with the excitement they wanted.

*Washington's Mark Brunell, 1991's Most Valuable Player.*

Late in the fourth quarter, the Ohio State Buckeyes held a 17-10 lead. Then USC took possession at its own thirty-

eight-yard line. At the controls for the Trojans was Pat Haden, who would later head to England as a Rhodes Scholar. Also playing was John McKay, a talented wide receiver and the son of the USC coach.

*A dramatic two-point conversion pass won the game for USC in 1975.*

The Trojans broke from their huddle. Haden took his drop and looked downfield. As he had hoped, McKay was open. And Haden delivered. The touchdown play brought USC within one point of the Buckeyes.

But time was running out. Knowing they would probably not get the ball back, the Trojans went for two on the extra point. It was a gamble. If they kicked the extra point, they had a tie. Failure on the two-point attempt meant a loss.

"We didn't come to play for a tie," Coach McKay said later.

The decision turned out to be the right one for the USC fans. Haden rolled right and connected with Sheldon Diggs in the end zone. USC had a dramatic 18-17 victory over the Buckeyes.

## BUNCE'S HOT HAND

Great Rose Bowl moments have often revolved around the leadership of quarterbacks. Don Bunce of Stanford was one such quarterback. Time was running out in the 1972 Rose Bowl game. The Stanford fans were roaring, hoping the Cardinal could march down the field and upset the favored Michigan Wolverines, who were trying to hold on to their slim lead.

*Quarterback sensation Mark Brunell in action.*

Bunce took the center snap, dropped back, and completed a thirteen-yard pass for a first down. Now there were sixty-five yards between him and the Michigan goal line.

Again he dropped back to pass. This time the completion was for sixteen yards. Now there were fifty-two yards to go.

Although Michigan knew Stanford was going to throw the ball, they couldn't stop Bunce's hot hand. Three more times he dropped back. Each time he completed his pass. He drove his team some eighty yards, but there wasn't time to try to reach the end zone. Onto the Rose Bowl turf came Stanford's placekicker Rod Garcia.

With fourteen seconds to play, Garcia kicked the game-winning field goal. Final score: Stanford 13, Michigan 12.

*USC's Todd Marinovich throws downfield during the 1990 game.*